The Tiara Club

✦ AT RUBY MANSIONS ✦

VIVIAN FRENCH

The Tiara Club

AT RUBY MANSIONS

Princess Olivia
AND THE
Velvet Cape

KATHERINE TEGEN BOOKS
HarperTrophy®
An Imprint of HarperCollinsPublishers

The Tiara Club at Ruby Mansions:
Princess Olivia and the Velvet Cape
Text copyright © 2008 by Vivian French
Illustrations copyright © 2008 by Orchard Books
www.harpercollinschildrens.com

Library of Congress Catalog Card Number: 2007905258
ISBN 978-0-06-143487-7

Typography by Amy Ryan

❖

First U.S. edition, 2008

For all of the hardworking princesses
at Hachette Children's Books,
with love and thanks
—V.F.

The Royal Palace Academy
for the Preparation of Perfect Princesses
(Known to our students as "The Princess Academy")

OUR SCHOOL MOTTO:
*A Perfect Princess always thinks of others before herself,
and is kind, caring, and truthful.*

Ruby Mansions offers a complete education for Tiara Club princesses with emphasis on the creative arts. The curriculum includes:

Innovative Ideas for our Friendship Festival

Designing Floral Bouquets (all thorns will be removed)

Ballet for Grace and Poise

*A visit to the Diamond Exhibition
(on the joyous occasion of Queen Fabiola's birthday)*

Our principal, Queen Fabiola, is present at all times, and students are in the excellent care of the head fairy godmother, Fairy G., and her assistant, Fairy Angora.

OUR RESIDENT STAFF & VISITING EXPERTS INCLUDE:

KING BERNARDO IV *(Ruby Mansions Governor)*

LADY ARAMINTA *(Princess Academy Matron)*

LADY HARRIS *(Secretary to Queen Fabiola)*

QUEEN MOTHER MATILDA *(Etiquette, Posture, and Flower Arranging)*

We award tiara points to encourage our
Tiara Club princesses toward the next level.
All princesses who earn enough points at Ruby
Mansions will attend a celebration ball, where
they will be presented with their Ruby Sashes.

Ruby Sash Tiara Club princesses are invited
to go on to Pearl Palace, our very special
residence for Perfect Princesses, where they may
continue their education at a higher level.

PLEASE NOTE:
Princesses are expected to arrive
at the Academy with a *minimum* of:

TWENTY BALL GOWNS
*(with all necessary hoops,
petticoats, etc.)*

TWELVE DAY-DRESSES

SEVEN GOWNS
*suitable for garden parties
and other special daytime
occasions*

TWELVE TIARAS

DANCING SHOES
five pairs

VELVET SLIPPERS
three pairs

RIDING BOOTS
two pairs

*Cloaks, muffs, stoles, gloves,
and other essential
accessories, as required*

Hello! I'm Princess Olivia, one of the Poppy Room Princesses, and I'm so pleased you're here too. Maybe you know Chloe, Jessica, Georgia, Lauren, and Amy? They're my best friends, and they're so nice! Not at all like the twins, Diamonde and Gruella. I know Perfect Princesses shouldn't say bad things about other princesses, but those two are so awful.

Chapter One

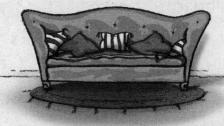

"Nothing exciting ever seems to happen anymore," Princess Jessica said gloomily. "We haven't had any balls or parties forever."

We were slumped on the sofas in the Recreation Room. It was true. It *did* feel as if school was going on and on, and every day was exactly the same.

"Should I go and look at the bulletin board?" I asked. That's where Lady Harris, our principal's assistant, puts up any invitations, or changes in classes, or anything else we should know about.

Princess Lauren yawned. "I looked on the way down here," she said. "The only new notice is about wearing sensible clothes. We've got to make sure we dress warmly when we go outside, because it's getting so cold."

"Do you think it'll snow soon?" Princess Amy asked hopefully.

"That would be fun."

I went to look out the window. "It does look quite cloudy—" I began, and then I stopped. Something very strange was happening in the courtyard outside. "Quick!" I gasped. "Look at this!"

My friends flew to join me at the window. We stared out at the Ruby Mansions footmen, who were hurrying around and carrying long planks of wood.

"What are they building?" Princess Chloe's eyes were wide.

"I think it's a stage," Jessica said thoughtfully.

Princess Georgia clapped her hands. "Something exciting must be happening! What do you think it'll be?"

"Maybe it'll be some kind of play," I suggested, and I hoped I was right. I really love acting.

The door to the Recreation Room opened and the horrible twins, Princess Diamonde and Princess Gruella, came sweeping in.

"Oooooh!" Diamonde trilled. "Look at the poor little Poppy Roomers peering out of the window! They must not have heard about the Grand Demonstration tomorrow."

Gruella sniffed. "*We* know all about it, don't we, Diamonde?"

"Of course." Diamonde gave us a snooty look. "King Rudolfo is such a good friend of Mommy's, so we know exactly what he's going to do. He's going to show us how Perfect Princesses should behave when a prince lays his cape on the ground in front of them."

"Why would a prince do that?"

Amy asked in surprise.

Gruella rolled her eyes. "Really!" she said. "Some princesses don't seem to know anything, do they, Diamonde? Should we tell her?"

Diamonde shook her head. "Certainly not. If Amy doesn't know something as simple as that, she shouldn't be here." And Diamonde stuck her nose in the air and flounced out of the room. Gruella hurried after her.

Jessica made a face as they slammed the door behind them. "They'll be absolutely awful tomorrow," she said. "I bet they will show off nonstop."

Amy was still looking puzzled. "Please, somebody tell me about this cape business!"

"It's a kind of traditional thing," Lauren explained. "If a Perfect Prince sees a Perfect Princess about to get her feet dirty, he's supposed to lay his cape down on the ground so she can step on that instead."

Georgia smiled at Amy's astonished face. "Silly, isn't it?"

"And actually, the cape makes it worse," Chloe said. "Soggy velvet is so hard to walk across. I expect that's why we're having a demonstration."

"Do you think we'll get to take turns?" Jessica asked.

"I hope so," I said. "That would be a lot of fun!" And this wonderful picture popped into my head of me floating across a crimson velvet cape, while a handsome prince bowed low in admiration.

Chapter Two

We were up bright and early the next morning, and we rushed down the stairs to breakfast so fast that Lady Harris, who was standing by the bulletin board, scolded us.

"Perfect Princesses do *not* jump the last three steps," she said firmly.

"Please go back to the first landing, and come down correctly!"

"We're so sorry, Lady Harris," Chloe said politely, and we trooped away back up the stairs to try again. This time, Lady Harris allowed us into the dining hall. We were just beginning to eat our oatmeal when Queen Fabiola, our principal, came marching in.

"Princesses!" she said loudly and waved her ear trumpet at us. "You have a great treat today! King Rudolfo is arriving this morning—"

"See? We *told* you!" Diamonde hissed in my ear.

"And there will be a Grand

Demonstration of Accepting Help with Grace and Elegance," Queen Fabiola went on.

Diamonde and Gruella folded their arms, and gave us an *I-told you-so!* stare, but they sat up straight when Queen Fabiola added, "And King Rudolfo will be bringing a group of princes from the Princes' Academy to help."

It was very funny—as soon as Queen Fabiola mentioned the princes, Diamonde and Gruella began to smooth their hair and straighten their dresses.

"Just look at Diamonde!" Jessica whispered. "What *is* she doing?"

Lauren gasped. "She's spilled tea on her dress. She did it on purpose!"

While we stared, Diamonde

raised her hand. "Excuse me, Your Majesty," she said. "May I be excused? I need to change my dress."

"What? What's that you say?" Queen Fabiola peered at Diamonde.

"What kind of mess? Oh, you silly girl! You've ruined your dress. Run along and change at once. I expect nothing but the very best from my princesses—in every way!"

As Diamonde hurried out of the

dining hall, we Poppy Roomers looked at one another. Georgia began to giggle. "She'll be back in her very best ball gown," she said. And she was absolutely right.

Ten minutes later, as we were filing out of the dining hall, Diamonde came back looking amazing in a pale green silk dress with tiny shoulder straps. It was beautiful—but it did look odd on a cold winter's day.

Gruella glared at her. "How come *you* got to change, and I didn't?" she asked.

"One has to look one's best for King Rudolfo and the princes,"

Diamonde said in a silly grown-up voice. "I'm going to say hello to them right now." And she tossed her hair back as she sailed ahead of us down the corridor.

Gruella made an angry growling

noise and stomped off after her.

"I wonder if Diamonde's noticed how cold it is," Lauren said. "She'll freeze and turn bright blue if she doesn't put something on over that dress."

And at that moment, Fairy G.,
our school Fairy Godmother,
appeared by the door that led out
to the courtyard where the stage
had been built.

"Princesses!" she boomed in her loudest voice. "It's very cold outside, so please make sure you're dressed properly." She caught sight of Diamonde making her way to the door in her silk dress, and her eyes widened. "Goodness me, Princess Diamonde! What *are* you wearing?"

Diamonde frowned. "I've made an effort to look nice for King Rudolfo. He's one of Mommy's best friends, you know."

Fairy G. raised her eyebrows. "If he's one of your mother's friends, he won't want you freezing to death. Go and put on something sensible."

Diamonde saw me watching, and she scowled as she stalked back to her room. Fairy G. shook her head and made sure the rest of us pulled on our boots and wrapped ourselves

in our cozy winter coats.

"King Rudolfo and the princes have just arrived," she told us. "Take your places in front of the stage. Once the demonstration is

over, there'll be hot chocolate and cinnamon toast for everyone." She paused and straightened Lauren's coat. "I'm sure I don't need to tell you to be on your best behavior, my dears. Queen Fabiola is very proud of her princesses, so don't let her down—especially in front of King Rudolfo and the princes!"

Chapter Three

I don't know how she did it, but when we came out into the court-yard, Diamonde was already sitting in the very front row. She was wearing a long green velvet coat that I had never seen before, and she did look very pretty. Gruella was beside her in her everyday winter coat looking grumpy.

As we walked over to the chairs and sat down, I couldn't help wondering why the demonstration had to be outside, but I soon found out. Two pages staggered onto the stage carrying buckets of water, followed

by two more with buckets of mud.

"Thank you, boys!" King Rudolfo came hurrying to check what they were doing. "Could you pour those over the middle of the stage, please?"

The pages nodded, and did as they were told.

"Excellent!" King Rudolfo rubbed his hands together and smiled. "Now, where are my volunteers?"

A long line of princes, looking handsome in satin coats and breeches, came marching out. Each of them was wearing a crimson velvet cape and a wide-brimmed hat, and as they came toward us, they swept off their hats and bowed. We tried to curtsey back. I wobbled a bit because I was very nervous, but Diamonde and Gruella sank into the deepest curtsies ever.

"Welcome to Ruby Mansions,"

Diamonde said in a sugary-sweet voice, and I could tell she was fluttering her eyelashes wildly.

The tallest prince, who was very handsome, gave Diamonde a dazzling smile.

"May I have the pleasure of asking you to be my partner in the demonstration?" he asked.

"Oh, of course," Diamonde said. As she stood up, she gave Gruella a triumphant smile.

King Rudolfo nodded approvingly. "Princess Diamonde, if I'm not mistaken? I know your mother, my dear."

Diamonde smiled coyly, and bobbed a curtsey.

But King Rudolfo had already turned to the other princes. "Come along," he said. "Invite some of these delightful princesses to help you."

The princes shuffled their feet and looked embarrassed, but at last they moved forward. A red-haired prince with bright blue eyes came to stand beside me.

He said, "Please, will you be my partner?"

"Thank you, Your Highness, I'd be delighted," I said and I walked with him to the stage.

As I passed Gruella, I heard her hiss, "That's not fair! He should have chosen me!" And she glared at me. I tried to ignore her, but I couldn't help seeing Diamonde giving her sister a sly little wink as I walked up the steps to join the others on the stage.

And I saw something else as well. Diamonde was wearing her sparkly party shoes instead of her boots. I wondered if Fairy G. had noticed.

"Time for the demonstration," King Rudolfo said. "We'll begin with Prince Ferdinand. Prince Ferdinand, remember everything I've taught you."

And I suddenly realized that Prince Ferdinand was *my* partner, and I hadn't the least idea what to do!

I swallowed hard. *It couldn't be that difficult,* I told myself. Prince Ferdinand would lay his cape down over the muddy mess in the middle of the stage, and I would sail across to the other side, and that would be that. He did look very nice. I looked at him hopefully, and waited for him to say something.

Nothing happened.

He opened and shut his mouth a couple of times, but no words came out. I tried to smile encouragingly, but that seemed to make things worse. He blushed bright red and mopped his face with a corner of his cape.

King Rudolfo made a *tsk-tsk* noise. "Dear me," he said. "Perhaps

we'd better ask Prince George instead."

The prince next to Diamonde bowed, and she looked very pleased. "Thank you, dear King Rudy," she said. "We'll do our best."

Diamonde stepped forward and as she passed me, she gave me a sharp push with her elbow. I completely lost my balance—and before I knew what was happening, I was sliding across the mud in the middle of the stage!

Chapter Four

I don't know how I didn't fall over. My arms flailed in all directions and I swayed this way and that way until I finally reached the other side and staggered onto the bare wooden boards. I must have looked about as un-princessy as ever, and I heard Diamonde and Gruella snickering—but at least I wasn't completely covered in mud. King Rudolfo was much too polite to laugh, but I could tell that nearly all the princes were trying really hard not to giggle. Prince Ferdinand was the only one who looked shocked instead of amused.

I turned and made my best curtsey to King Rudolfo. "Please excuse me, Your Majesty," I said. "I'm so very sorry. I slipped."

"Princess Olivia! What do you think you're doing?" It was Queen Fabiola. She was waving her ear trumpet in the air as she stormed her way toward me.

My knees began to tremble. She
sounded furious!

"I came to see how my princesses were enjoying the demonstration, and I find you spinning about in the middle of the stage like a circus clown. What do you have to say for yourself?"

I stared down at the wooden boards and wished I could sink into them. I couldn't explain that Diamonde had pushed me without being a terrible tattletale, so I whispered, "Excuse me, Your

Majesty, I lost my balance."

"I can't hear you, child. You're muttering dreadfully. And such ridiculous behavior! I'm ashamed of you." Queen Fabiola looked like a thundercloud. "Go and wait outside my study. I shall speak to you later."

I could feel my face burning as I hurried off the stage, and I almost ran back into Ruby Mansions. Behind me, I could hear Queen Fabiola suggesting that everyone take a brisk walk around the court-yard to get warm before Prince George and Diamonde began the demonstration.

I was afraid I might cry—and I was determined not to. That would really make Diamonde happy.

I sniffed hard as I walked along the empty hallway, and wondered what was going to happen to me. Would I be given hundreds of minus tiara points or would it be something even worse? I stood outside Queen Fabiola's door and fished in my pocket for a tissue.

Then someone coughed behind me and a hand passed me a snow-white handkerchief.

I turned around—and my mouth fell wide open while I stared. I must have looked like a goldfish, because Prince Ferdinand began to smile.

"What are you doing here?" I asked. "I'm in disgrace!"

"It wasn't your fault," he said firmly. "I saw that horrible girl push you. I tried to tell your principal, but she wouldn't listen. She waved me to one side, so I thought I'd follow you, and"—he hesitated—"and I also wanted to say I'm really sorry I was so useless. If I hadn't had such awful stage fright,

none of this would have happened."

"That's very nice of you," I said. "And it's okay. It really is."

Prince Ferdinand shook his head. "It isn't. Normally I'm one of the best in the class, but I get so nervous in front of an audience. Especially when it's girls—hey!" He suddenly looked cheerful. "Why don't I show you now? I won't be nervous in front of you."

"What?" I couldn't believe what I was hearing. "You mean, show me how to walk across a cape?"

"Exactly!" Prince Ferdinand bowed deeply, swept off his velvet cape, and laid it on the floor in front of me. "Dear Princess Olivia, may I have the pleasure of assisting you across this extremely muddy puddle?"

I couldn't help smiling. "Thank you, Your Highness," I said in my

very best Perfect Princess voice. "I would be most grateful." And I tip-toed gracefully across the velvet cape to the other side, while Prince Ferdinand waited patiently.

"Perfect!" He gave me a huge smile. "I knew you'd be a star!"

"Of course she is!" boomed a voice from the other end of the hallway, and there was Fairy G. She came stomping toward us, and Prince Ferdinand looked at her nervously.

"It's okay," I whispered. "Fairy

G. is wonderful!"

"I may be wonderful," Fairy G. bellowed, "but could you please explain why you have decided to conduct the most excellent demonstration all by yourselves in the hallway?"

All at once I remembered what had happened, and I hung my head. Prince Ferdinand stood up very straight.

"Unfortunately, Princess Olivia almost slipped on the stage, Your Fairyness," he said. "She waved her arms like a windmill when she was trying to save herself. Her principal thought she was showing off, and sent her indoors, but it wasn't her fault. She was pushed by another princess—I was standing right beside her when she did it. And Olivia's much too nice to tattle, so I'm telling you instead."

"I see," Fairy G. said and her

eyes began to twinkle. "Well . . .
perhaps we should go back outside
and see how things are going." And
she marched the two of us back
down the hall and out into the
courtyard.

We were just in time to see

Diamonde tripping in her sparkly party shoes. As she fell, she grabbed Prince George, and he slipped as well—and the two of them fell half on the cape, and half in the mud.

"Oh! Oh! Oh!" Diamonde screamed. "You stupid boy! You've

ruined my dress!" And as she picked herself up, everyone could see her beautiful ball gown was completely covered in mud. Diamonde screamed again and ran off the stage and into the school, slamming the door behind her. Everyone began to talk at once, but Fairy G. stepped forward and held up her wand.

"I think," she boomed, "we'd better start again. Let's go back to the beginning!"

She waved her wand and tiny golden sparkles flew in every direction—and all of a sudden Prince Ferdinand and I were back

on the stage. We rubbed our eyes
and stared at each other, and then
King Rudolfo spoke.

"Time for the demonstration,"

he said. "We'll begin with Prince Ferdinand. Prince Ferdinand, remember everything I've taught you."

And Prince Ferdinand gave me an enormous grin as he stepped forward.

"Dear Princess Olivia, may I have the pleasure of assisting you across this extremely muddy puddle?"

"Thank you, Your Highness," I said. "I would be most grateful." And—guess what? I tiptoed across just as gracefully as I had when we were in the school hallway, and everyone clapped so loudly!

And from the back of the audience, Queen Fabiola waved her ear trumpet triumphantly. "Give Princess Olivia twenty tiara points, Fairy G.!" she called.

"Certainly, Your Majesty," Fairy G. said and she gave me a tiny wink.

It was only after I'd gone back to my seat that I realized things weren't exactly the same as they had been. Diamonde was missing, but a couple of moments later, she came hurrying out of the school, and slipped quietly into a seat. As she sat down, I found myself looking at her feet—and she was wearing her boots, just like the rest of us.

Chapter Five

*I*t was a while before everyone had a turn on the stage. But as soon as it was over, a group of pages brought out huge trays of hot chocolate and cinnamon toast. It was just what we needed to warm us up! We were finishing our last sips of chocolate when King Rudolfo strode back onto the stage and clapped his hands to get our attention.

"Princes and princesses," he said. "Queen Fabiola and I are delighted with your work, so we have arranged for the Princes' Academy Musicians to join us. As soon as the stage has been swept clean, they will take their positions and play for you—and if that doesn't warm you up, nothing will!"

And he was right. The musicians began with the bounciest polka you've ever heard—and who do you think was the first to be invited to dance?

Yes! Me!

Prince Ferdinand seized my hand and whirled me across the

courtyard, and it was so much fun.

"I knew you'd be good at dancing when I saw you sliding across the stage trying not to fall over," he said with a grin. "And I never get

stage fright when I'm dancing!"

"Me neither," I said, and we twirled around and around until we were out of breath. . . .

And as I went to sit down with

my wonderful friends from the Poppy Room, I knew I was the luckiest princess in the whole wide world.

And I'm lucky in another way too—because you're my very special friend!

What happens next?

FIND OUT IN

✦ *Princess Lauren* ✦
⤳ AND THE ⤲
Diamond Necklace ✦

Greetings, dear princess! I'm Lauren,
by the way. And did you know
I'm a Poppy Room Princess?
Chloe, Jessica, Georgia, Olivia,
and Amy are my very best
friends, just like you—and I'm so glad we're
all at Ruby Mansions together. Do you go on
field trips at your school? We do, and we
have so much fun—just as long as Diamonde
and Gruella don't spoil everything. You've met
them, I'm sure. They're the horrible twins. . . .

Visit all your favorite

The Tiara Club

Tiara Club princesses!

The Tiara Club
AT SILVER TOWERS

for games, puzzles, and more fun!

You are cordially invited to the Royal Princess Academy.

Introducing the new class of princesses at Ruby Mansions

Katherine Tegen Books
An Imprint of HarperCollinsPublishers

HarperTrophy®
An Imprint of HarperCollinsPublishers